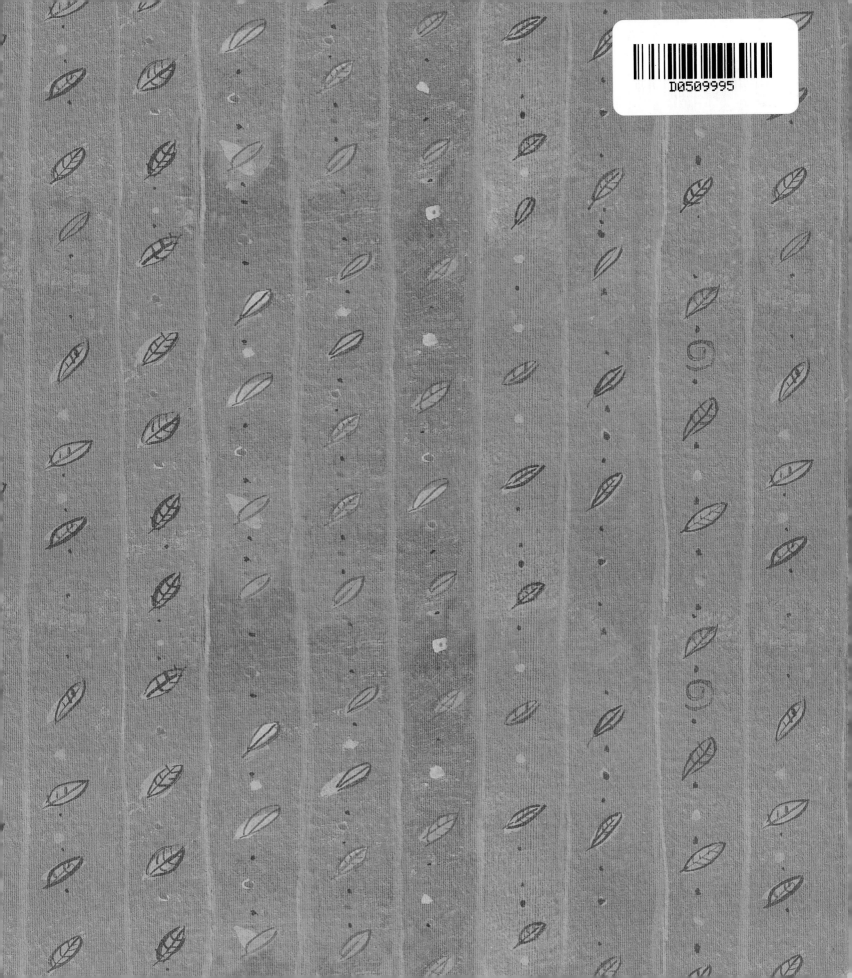

To Amy, Lara and Sophie Maya,
who are all fabulous – LP

LITTLE TIGER PRESS
An imprint of Magi Publications
1 The Coda Centre,
189 Munster Road, London SW6 6AW
www.littletigerpress.com

First published in Great Britain 2010
This edition published 2010
Text and Illustrations copyright © Liz Pichon 2010
Liz Pichon has asserted her rights to be identified as the author and
illustrator of this work under the Copyright, Designs and Patents Act, 1988
A CIP catalogue record for this book
is available from the British Library
All rights reserved

ISBN 978-1-84506-985-8
Printed in China
10 9 8 7 6 5 4 3 2 1

The Real Story of Cinderella and the Ugly Sisters

Liz Pichon

LITTLE TIGER PRESS

London

Once upon a time, Cinderella lived with her two very ugly sisters. Cinderella was **beautiful** and gorgeous . . .

but she was also a miserable
little madam.

Her ugly sisters were NOT a pretty sight,
but they were always kind and cheerful . . .

even when Cinderella
was NASTY!

One day an invitation arrived from the palace
to attend a **fabulous** ball. The ugly sisters were thrilled!

"Let's scrub up and put on our dancing shoes," they cheered!
  "Why bother?" Cinderella moaned.
"Besides, who'll dance with you two ugly monsters?"
And she stomped off to watch TV.

Cinderella really was a stroppy little madam!

Anti-Pong Spray

Fur Cream

The Two Princes invite Cinderella and the Ugly Sisters to come to a fabulous ball at the Grand Palace. Please bring your dancing shoes!

Eau de Cat

Moustache Removal Cream

The ugly sisters felt sorry for Cinderella. "She needs to get out more and have some fun!" they purred.

Quick – we need help!

What are we going to do with her?

So the ugly sisters picked up the phone and called . . .

...the Fairy Godfather!

"Stop being such a grump and get ready for the ball!" he bellowed.

"No chance!" Cinderella sulked.

"We'll see about that!" said the Fairy Godfather. Then he waved his magic wand and changed Cinderella instantly into . . .

"And don't even think of leaving the ball early," the Fairy Godfather told her, "or you'll turn into a **pumpkin!**"

And he waved his wand once more,

sending them off to the ball in style.

until she started moaning
(which didn't take very long).

Cinderella **pushed** past Prince Buff and
accidentally (on purpose) stamped on his foot.

She **ignored** Prince Hunk and
scoffed all the **cakes** instead.

Then she threw off her glass slippers
and left the ball well **before midnight** . . .

I'm off!

which turned out to be a BIG mistake . . .

Meanwhile, Prince Buff and Prince Hunk fell madly in love with the two ugly sisters.

And after a whirlwind romance . . .

the princes and the two ugly sisters got married in
a sumptuous double wedding. Everyone was
fabulously happy.

Whooppee!

Well, everyone apart from Cinderella . . .

... who lived **grumpily** ever after!